Tommaso

and

the Missing Line

by

matteo pericoli

Alfred A. Knopf New York

To the memory of nonna Mimia

There once was a little boy
named Tommaso.
He always kept
a drawing in his pocket.

One day a strange thing happened:
one of the lines in Tommaso's drawing
was gone—disappeared.

"Where did my line go?"
he asked his mother.

The drawing was only a drawing,
but Tommaso loved it.
He had made it all by himself
just a few months before.

It showed a house on a hill,
a tall tree and some mountains.
And two people—
him and his grandma.

THIS IS THE
DRAWING

"What happened to my line?"
Tommaso asked his mother
one more time.

"What line, sweet pea?
What's on your mind?"

"The line of the hill, mamma," he said.
"It was right here, I drew it myself.
You see? It's not there anymore!"

"It must be there, Tommaso,"
his mother replied.
"Look carefully, my dear—
lines don't just disappear!"

But the line was indeed gone,
so Tommaso—in a hurry—
left his house in search of it.

"Where did my line go?"
he asked the old dog
wandering past his building.

The old dog kept trotting by
without saying a word.
He was wearing the only line
he'd ever known, his leash.

"Hey, Gregorio! Have you seen my line?"
Tommaso asked the mechanic.

"You are missing a line, my friend?
What about the antenna
on the car over there?"

"No, no. That's not the one I mean."

Tommaso kept walking
until he ran into a cat
very busy with his nap.

He stopped and asked,
"Hello, mister cat.
Sorry to wake you,
but I can't seem to find
a line that belongs in my drawing.
Have you seen it?"

The cat didn't even bother
to open both eyes.
He had better things to worry about.

In fact, without saying a word,
he fell right back asleep
and dreamt of his own favorite line—
his tail.

"Maybe Luigi knows,"
Tommaso thought.

He stopped in front of Luigi's barbershop.
"Luigi! Have you seen my line?"

"Hold on a moment, little fellow,"
Luigi answered.
"Why don't you tell me what happened
while I cut your hair?"

So Tommaso explained to Luigi
everything about his drawing—
that he drew it at his grandma's house
on a hot summer afternoon
while she was preparing the evening meal.
That the cicadas outside were so loud,
and her simmering sauce
filled the air with a delicious smell.
And that every time he looked at his drawing,
he could remember all of this.

"And now the line of the hill is gone!"
he added at the end.

"Why don't you draw it again, Tommaso?
After all," the barber said,
"a line is just a line."

"Well," Tommaso answered
as he turned to Luigi,
"that's what it may seem to you,
but my line is not just *any* line.
I want to find the very one that is missing,
and I don't want any other!"

"If you don't sit down, Tommaso,
I can't cut your hair," Luigi said.

And then Luigi added,
"You know, my boy,
the only lines that I have ever seen
fall by the thousands
on this floor every day.
Some are straight, some are curly,
some are dark, some are light,
some are even red!
And," he went on,
"none of them looks like yours."

Tommaso thanked Luigi and walked out.

As he passed by Annamaria's café,
he heard a train whistle.

"Of course,"
he told himself.
"That's what I will do!
I'll go visit nonna.
She must know. She always knows."

So Tommaso got on a train heading south.

As the train pulled out,
he began to wonder
about his missing line.

"Where did my line go?"
Tommaso asked himself.

"How could the line of the hill,
of all lines,
disappear from my drawing?
And why?"

"Mamma says that
lines don't just disappear,
but mine did."
And he looked at his drawing
one more time.

"I wonder if my line
was as real as Gregorio's antenna
or the hair Luigi cuts every day."

At last, Tommaso
arrived at his destination.
From the station
he walked to his grandma's house.

The house looked
as beautiful as always.
The cicadas were not as loud,
for the summer had turned into fall.
And his grandma was outside,
picking fresh figs.

"Tommaso,"
she said as she hugged him,
"how come this surprise visit?"

"Do you remember, nonna,
the drawing I made this summer?"

"I certainly do,"
she answered.

And he told her how
the line of the hill
was gone, vanished.

"I went searching for it all day
before I came to see you.
Do you have any idea
where it may have gone?"

"Oh, that is indeed
very strange," she told him.
"I remember you making the
drawing right next to me.
And I remember those graceful lines.
They seemed so real—
they seemed to be coming
straight from the hill,
from the house, from the tree."

"Yes. But now
the line of the hill is gone!"

"If it's not in your drawing, Tommaso,"
his grandma continued,
"it must have gone somewhere.
And I think I know where."

"Do you, really?"

"Of course. Come with me."

She took Tommaso by the hand,
and together they walked
to the bottom of the hill.
They turned around and looked up.

Though the colors were not as bright,
and the air not as warm,
the view was the very one
that Tommaso remembered.

"Here you go,"
his grandma told him.
"Look up at the hill."

And there it was,
Tommaso's missing line,
as real as he always
remembered it.

A BORZOI BOOK PUBLISHED BY ALFRED A. KNOPF

Copyright © 2008 by Matteo Pericoli

All rights reserved. Published in the United States by Alfred A. Knopf,
an imprint of Random House Children's Books, a division of Random House, Inc., New York.

Knopf, Borzoi Books, and the colophon are registered trademarks of Random House, Inc.

Visit us on the Web! www.randomhouse.com/kids

Educators and librarians, for a variety of teaching tools, visit us at www.randomhouse.com/teachers

Library of Congress Cataloging-in-Publication Data
Pericoli, Matteo.
Tommaso and the missing line / Matteo Pericoli. — 1st ed.
p. cm.
Summary: When Tommaso discovers that a line is missing from his favorite drawing, he goes looking for it all around
town and notices many lines he never saw before.
ISBN 978-0-375-84102-6 (trade) — ISBN 978-0-375-94102-3 (lib. bdg.)
[1. Line (Art)—Fiction. 2. Drawing—Fiction. 3. Lost and found possessions—Fiction.] I. Title.
PZ7.P4276Tom 2008
[E]—dc22
2007043518

The text of this book is set in 16-point Roice.
The lines in the drawings of this book were created using a dip pen and china ink on white paper.

MANUFACTURED IN MALAYSIA
December 2008
10 9 8 7 6 5 4 3 2 1

First Edition

Random House Children's Books supports the First Amendment and celebrates the right to read.